T0072500

The London Times

Book One
of the
Caldwell Series

Angela Lacey

Order this book online at www.trafford.com
or email orders@trafford.com

Most Trafford titles are also available at major online book retailers.

THIS BOOK IS A WORK OF FICTION, any similarities of names,
characters, places, events, people, or localities is strictly coincidental, are
used fictitiously, or they are a product of the author's imagination!

Print information available on the last page

ISBN: 978-1-4907-5570-0 (sc)
ISBN: 978-1-4907-5569-4 (e)

Trafford rev. 06/10/2015

Trafford
PUBLISHING® www.trafford.com
North America & international
toll-free: 1 888 232 4444 (USA & Canada)
fax: 812 355 4082

A New Beginning

"Okay, okay, first things first, let me run through a mental checklist here; I am all cleaned up, have my conservative dress clothes on, my hair is curled, my makeup is also conservative, I look pretty good. Paper and pens, check, computer on, speakers on. I have logged into SKYPE, now, all that remains is to await a *Mr. Stuart Simon* to call. This is my second interview with *The London Times*, ooo, I am so excited. Please God, let me get this." Brandy said aloud to herself, nervously. She had taken her anti-anxiety pill earlier, but it still had not kicked in.

Bloop, bloop, went her computer. The normally blue Skype icon on her computer screen was glowing a bright orange now, indicating a call or message.

"This is it," Brandy told herself, "I've got this! I can do this, I have been on interviews before."

Brandy switched on her camera and turned up her speaker, "Good morning." She said excitedly.

"Hello, my name is Stuart Simon, I'm the Human Resources Generalist that is to interview you today for your second interview with *The London Times* if you are Brandy Goshen?" asked the cute man, cheerfully.

"Yes, I am Brandy, how are you this morning Mr. Simon?" said Brandy nervously.

"I am fine, so good to meet you. Well, let's get right down to our interview, shall we?" he asked, "and please, call me Stuart."

"Okay, and you may call me Brandy." she replied, more confidently this time.

"You can relax Brandy, this won't take long. So, where do you work now, or what was your last job?" inquired Stuart.

"I currently work at the News Journal, it's the local newspaper and I am a columnist."

"And why do you want to leave this position, I see here on your resume' that you have been with that company for a decade now." added Stuart.

"I feel I have learned all I can learn in this position. I also want a change of scenery, plus I no longer feel challenged here, it is just time to move on for me." Brandy added.

"Now, you do realize that if you are offered and accept this position that it will require you to move to London, and that you would need to be able to start with very little notice, right?"

"Oh, yes. I was explained all that in the conversation I had yesterday with Rebecca from your Human Resources. I told her I was fine with doing all of that." Explained Brandy.

"Do you have any questions for me?" asked Stuart.

"No, I understood that I will receive two thousand dollars as moving expenses, and a few weeks to find a place and get moved to London." recited Brandy.

"Well then, if you are prepared to do all she had asked of you, I am now prepared to formally offer you the Online Copy Editor's position with *The London Times.*" he offered.

Stuart was very cute in Brandy's opinion, and she liked the way his voice sounded as well. She figured he was probably already married, or involved or whatever. All the good ones usually were.

"Ms. Goshen, would you like the position, Ms. Goshen?" Stuart repeated.

"Oh, yes, yes, I would love it, I am honored, thank you so much." Brandy had been in a bit of a daze with all of the excitement, she has lost herself for a brief moment.

"You are to report to the Human Resources office at 8am local London time, on Monday, three weeks from this coming Monday, will that be doable for you?" asked Stuart.

"Oh, yes, I will be there sir."

Brandy couldn't wait to get finished with that interview, she wanted to tell someone so badly that she had gotten the position of her dreams.

No sooner had she logged off her computer did her phone ring, it was her mother. "Brandy, did your interview take place? How did it go?"

"Hi, yes Mom, I had it, it went so well. I got the job, I start two weeks from this Monday, and I can't wait. Oh you are gonna have to help me Mom. I need to get FrouFrou over to you, you are still gonna keep him right? And I will need to go and arrange to have boxes shipped, I am not taking everything, just stuff I won't likely be able to replace easily there. Oh, I am so worked up Mom, be happy for me." Brandy sounded almost giddy.

"Brandy, I am happy for you Hun, I will miss you like crazy, but I know you have to go. After that creep Tray cheated on you the way he did, you probably will be glad for the fresh start won't you?" Mom was concerned, and it showed in her voice.

The move was almost seamless. Brandy had already packed all of her belongings, so she took the boxes to the post office to be shipped to a storage unit in London, which she paid for over the phone. Her dog went to her mother, her ex-boyfriend had moved on, and that was that. The lease had just ended for her apartment, which made this an especially perfect time for her to move. She was all smiles as she boarded the plane.

The London version of English was very different than what she was used to back in the States. Londoners had their own vocabulary. Every time she learned a new term for something, she tried to put it into practice right away. *Loo* meant bathroom, but they could also call it a water closet or toilet, a *lorry* was a truck, *crisps* were potato chips, *biscuits* were cookies, *the tube* was a subway tunnel, a *flat* was an apartment, and that was just for starters. Also, for emergencies, they dialed 999 or 211 instead of the 911 that was used back home in America. So many things were different here, it would take some adjustment.

Her first task upon getting to London would be to secure a flat, and perhaps a flatmate. Preferably near the London Times office, where she would be working, or at least near the tube entrance or a bus stop. Just across from the Times was a little café.

This day, she was freezing from the icy rain, and stopped in to have a snack and a cup of hot tea. Looking at the vast selection on the menu, Brandy had a hard time deciding which she would have. So much to choose from! "Taking a tea" was an event for a person in England. There were actually three teas in a single British day: Afternoon Tea, Cream Tea, and High Tea. They each had something that would differentiate them one from the other. She finally settled on just a scone with jam with clotted crème to dip in and an Earl Grey tea. There were no sandwiches involved here, so it would not replace a full meal. This was considered a Cream Tea.

The server's name was Lucille Caldwell or "Lucy". Now, Lucy was a very chatty person by nature. Lucy (who waitressed when she was not day dreaming) told her of the apartment where she lived, and that she was actually looking for a flatmate herself! Could things really be this easy for Brandy? Was moving here to Europe truly going to be all she'd had her heart set on?

Luck was on her side again, or so it would seem. They exchanged information and Lucy promised to call Brandy that evening to allow her to see the place.

That night, when Lucy finished her double shift, she called Brandy. "Let's meet at the pub here on the corner. I want to introduce you to my friends. Some of them live in the building. One guy, Alan, even works at the paper, not sure doing what." offered Lucy.

"I will be right over," Brandy stated. Finally some excitement, she thought.

Later, at the pub, Brandy had no trouble spotting Lucy. She was standing among a crowd of rowdy people, center of attention, and loving every minute of it.

"Hey, there she is now," said Lucy, "Brandy, we're all over here! Come and meet my friends." Scanning the crowd to take it all in, Brandy could not believe her eyes. Sitting among them was none other than her ex-boyfriend; Tray.

What in the world was he doing here in London? Her hands trembled at the shock of seeing him here. He worked for a paper back home. They had gone out for just less than two years. He had left her for a French woman... *Has he moved here for her?* she wondered.

She rescanned the group, looking for someone Tray might go out with. She knew his type, hell, she was his type!

Trace "Tray" Anderson liked redheads and rarely dated anyone who wasn't. They had been columnist together back in the States, and had always gotten along well, until they decided to move in together, that's when their issues began.

Brandy used to find Tray's looks disarming. Even now that they were no longer going out, she still found him incredibly attractive. He was the kind of good looking that could render a girl speechless and weak in the knees with just a glance. He had that certain je ne sais quoi or that little something about him.

Now he was here? Well great! That's what she got for not keeping her plans to move private, now everyone and everything she had escaped in the States could follow her!

But wait a minute, what are the chances he would have ended up in London? His lady friend was French, not English. Still, the two countries weren't that far apart, it seemed feasible to her somehow. Brandy thought, as she tried to make sense of it all in her mind. "Well, for the love of all that is holy, Brandy Goshen, as I live and breathe," Tray spoke louder than he really needed, to be heard over the crowd; "what the hell are *you* doing here? Thought I left you back in the dust of the US of A?"

Funny, she was wondering the same thing herself. Just then, one of the prettiest ladies in the bar, a brunette, spoke up and said, "Tray honey, who is this?" She put her hand on his shoulder in such a way that it told every woman for miles around that this was her man and no one had better try to take him.

"A brunette?" she thought. "Hmmm, maybe he had changed."

"Oh, where are my manners?" asked Tray. "Brandy this is Elizabeth, Liz this is Brandy, I know her from the paper back in the US."

"Hi, nice to meet you." Each lady smiled a smile of obligation as they shook hands, but the brunette was shooting daggers as she did.

"*Well, so much for a fresh start out here.*" thought Brandy. She could feel herself getting angry. From her vantage point, she could see that the hand on Tray's shoulder had now slid down onto his chest, just over his peck.

"Trace Jethro Anderson!" she heard herself shout. She had no idea why she felt even remotely like she still had a say over whom he was dating. But somehow, at that moment, seeing him in London after leaving him behind in the US; she did. And evidently, she also had no control over whether or not she said it aloud.

"*Maybe things would have been different if our breakup had been official, or if we had parted ways due to not getting along, or had not being in love in the first place, but none of those had been the case.*" thought Brandy

Tray barely looked up when she shouted his name. It was clear he was secure in whatever relationship he had with this Liz woman.

Just a few months earlier, Brandy and Tray had been living together. He was getting ready for work one morning and was in the shower. His cell (which was in the living room) beeped. Brandy went and picked it up to take it to him. She assumed it was his job calling. He *had* been working late all week on a big project.

Then she saw that it was not a voice mail, but a text message. Maybe she shouldn't have looked, but something told her to. It was from a lady at his job who didn't live far from work. She was asking when he was going to be stopping over again, and if she could see him *that* night? And she said how much fun she'd had when they were together *last* night, and that she would see him at work today. She'd figured out his game. She would have had to be completely dense not to get it.

Later that day, he had called Brandy up out of the blue and said he had met someone else, was not coming back to her, and that he would be by shortly to get his things from what had been their place.

That was it. There had been no drama, no fight, no words, nothing. Brandy had been so numbed, by those words, she could not even think. If this was what he wanted to do or try, then she would be happy for him. Just like that, it was over. He was out the door as quickly as he had entered. Looking around, you could not tell Tray had ever even been there.

Next had come her move to London, and although her mom had kept her updated with any back home gossip that she knew, it didn't tell Brandy much. The breakup had only been a few months ago, but it seemed like an eternity. And now *this*, what was Brandy thinking?

She never meant to come at this lady and Tray with both guns aimed and loaded. He had a right to move on from her, just the same as she had a right to move on from him.

But she hadn't yet.

Brandy would normally have just said something smartalecky, and left it at that, but she thought it best to keep quiet and say nothing. She had no words anyway, which was so not like her. She was not here for this "Liz" person, or even for Tray for that matter anyway, she had only wanted to have a few drinks and go see the flat, if that worked for Lucy.

"Oh my God, you guys know each other?" chimed in Lucy. "And all the way from America, what are the odds?" she added.

This day was not turning out quite the way Brandy had imagined, or hoped even, and she planned to do something about that right away. But maybe a drink first?

A waiter approached and took their orders. Brandy had ordered a light beer, she truly wanted to chug hers down and get the hell out of there, but she couldn't do that to Lucy.

"Lucy," she whispered, "any chance we can go see your place before it gets too late? I don't want to be out all hours, in case I still have more looking to do."

Out of the group, there were maybe eight guys, half of which were on their third beer at least and she had not even finished her first. *Was it possible several were even getting drunk already?* She thought. *Maybe the beer here was stronger than the beer back home?*

Now some of the guys were starting to get a little too familiar with her and with some of the other female patrons in the bar.

One of the men, Joseph, who was not an invited part of their group, reached over and began cupping one of Brandy's breast. Before she knew it, she had decked him but good right in the nose.

He was now bleeding and she was sorry that he was, but he deserved it. She threw a bunch of napkins at him. Lucy was laughing hysterically. She hoped she hadn't broken it, but if she had, he had received what he deserved.

If she wanted to leave before, now she really wanted to get out of there! Her other concern was; how she would ever be able to get Lucy home if Lucy got drunk? Brandy didn't know the way to the address she had scrawled on her paper receipt. Brandy sighed. Maybe this whole move had been a bad idea after all. Thankfully, Lucy was ready to leave herself. "I can play around with these blokes any time," said Lucy, "and besides, I am feeling a little tipsy, maybe we should get going?"

And just like that, they were leaving that awful scene. She decided she would drive, which was a good thing, since, come to find out, Lucy had no car. Brandy also did not want to leave her car there for the night.

As Brandy drove to the scribbled address following Lucy's tipsy directions, she couldn't stop thinking about Tray's soft laugh and the way Liz's hand had touched him so possessively.

"What a bloody mess," she muttered.

2

The Flat

It turned out that the flat was rather sweet inside, and the room she had to rent was everything Lucy had said it would be. Finally, something was going right.

Given the fact that Brandy was now feeling an enormous sense of exhaustion due to that whole bar scene and having to see Tray again, she thought it over and did a quick mental calculation in her mind.

"Nice girl, cheap rent, clean home, and furnished room? She thought. *"*I'll take it!" she told Lucy aloud. Her mind was made up. The flat wasn't far from work, making it all the more convenient.

That's when Brandy's cell phone rang. It was her mom calling from back home. "Lucy Sweetheart, it's your FrouFrou, well Hun, he passed early this morning in his sleep

Her poodle *was* old and its death *was* inevitable. Still, it was never something you are prepared to hear.

Well, that's two negative things today; the first was clearly meeting up with Tray, and now the death of her beloved poodle FrouFrou. Her mother had always told her bad things happen in sets of threes. What next? Brandy worried.

Brandy really liked her new writing position at *The Times*. It was just a copy editor's position, but she was also given the option to do the column "Auntie Agony," the English equivalent of America's "Dear Abby" column. She was not interested in writing for that, though. She had to give her opinion often enough in everyday life, and she did not look forward to that being her job as well.

Sales in the paper version of the newspaper were down industry wide, but in light of the boost in sales of the online version of the paper. New online positions were becoming available, and at a time when many were losing their jobs, at least she had a job.

Her particular position had to be practically reinvented for her. She did a lot of her work online; namely editing, writing, rewriting, and submitting photos to go with the articles.

Anyone who did not love writing and news as much as she did would likely have tired of it after a day. Even when working from home, Brandy had to do the typical office worker ergonomics, such as reminding herself not to sit too long, to look away from the computer screen, do stretches, and get up now and then so as not to get a stiff neck or sore back. Sometimes she just plain needed a distraction from all the writing, but other than that she loved it.

Her flatmate, Lucy, had also put in an application at the Times for an administrative position on the first floor. It wasn't much, but it certainly paid better than the café and required far fewer hours. *Having a passenger will certainly make the commute more interesting*, thought Brandy.

Brandy had already known that a position was opening downstairs months ago. That's when Shelly, a knockout, became the new secretary on her floor. Shelly had taken the position of working for Stuart Simon. This left the clerical position open.

To Lucy's great surprise, (but largely due to Brandy's excellent recommendation) Lucy got the job. Having a passenger will certainly make the commute more interesting, Brandy thought.

Stuart was a kind man, good looking, and made very good money working for the Times. He seemed quite a catch for someone. As the paper's News Editor, Stuart worked on the less prominent pages rather than the headlines. When it came to publishing and deadlines, he decided what made it to print, and what made it to the trash.

Brandy reported to Stuart, and Stuart himself was very happy to have her working there. He was greatly attracted to her, and was trying to get up the nerve to ask her out. He would need to clear it with HR first, of course, but he didn't think they would have a problem with it. After all, he had made good friends over the years with several of the HR Senior Execs.

He would ask her out, and if she said yes, there should be no problem. He thought she would as they had shared a couple of moments, nothing illicit, but just some passing glances, some flirty moments. Enough that he felt his courage bolstered to ask her out, with some reasonable degree of confidence that she would say yes.

Brandy primarily worked online, sometimes even from home. That is what she liked best about her position, if she didn't feel like getting dressed up or going in, she didn't usually have to.

As a member of their online staff, she produced Web content, flash animations, and edited Web-only features and she love it. Basically, she added pictures to the words which were sometimes hers and other times submitted by other writers.

Brandy was a whiz on the computer. In times past, the paper had been in print form only. Now that the company was going online for so much of their material presentation, they needed someone well versed in copy, as well as in uploading pictures for the accompaniment of such written material. She knew how to do all that and more.

The articles were partially written already by the time she got her hands on them, but she would still need to add the artwork, pictures, and graphics to increase volume and overall attractiveness of the article.

It was mid-February, and of course the office was all abuzz with the usual Valentine's Day gossip about who fancied whom. Therefore, it was no real surprise when she arrived to work on February the thirteenth to see a card and red heart shaped box on her desk.

She was pretty sure she knew who they were from; Tray, she thought. Perhaps he had decided he was going to ask her out again. For just a fleeting moment, she felt a charge of excitement. But why? She didn't want to go out with him again. She wasn't that crazy after all. They had tried it together, and it had not worked out. That ship had sailed, and they were not on it. Nope! She hadn't even opened the card yet, and she already knew that she had to turn him down.

Brandy knew how illicit Tray could be in his writings from their past time together, so she took the card into the loo to open it lest someone come along and read something over her shoulder she shouldn't see.

She used her nail file and slid it under the seal of the red envelope. Slowly she pulled the card from the inside, opened it, and immediately let her eyes go to the end of the card to see the signature, "Yours, Stuart" it read.

Brandy frowned in disappointment. She did like him, a lot actually. Stuart was a great guy. He would never have cheated on her the way Tray did. These things she said in her mind almost as much to convince herself as to review her feelings.

Brandy's mind was even a little too fickle for her own liking. Why couldn't she just hate Tray like any other woman in her right mind would? Why did she have to only remember the good in people and forget the negative? That was one of her best and worse characteristics.

But then, really good looking guys had all the girls after them, and it was much more difficult for them to remain true to just one.

With the initial shock regarding the card's sender now over, she quickly read through the contents of the note. It was an invitation to go out with Stuart that very evening.

About that time, just as Stuart was approaching to confirm their dinner plans, who should also arrive at her desk with a half dead, sorry-looking, single rose, but Tray.

"Hey", he said, handing her the rose, "Happy V-day!" She had never fancied that expression "V-day" Yuck, she could well imagine what the V was that most guys were thinking of, and that was a crude thought to be celebrating.

"Oh, thanks Tray," she said lightheartedly, "I will have to get some water for it... I guess." Of course she was also thinking she may need first aid or the power of the resurrection, that rose had clearly seen better days and possibly other vases from the looks of it.

Speaking in a low tone, Tray continued; "So, I just wanted to let you know that Liz and I - well, we broke up."

"So sorry to hear that! When did this happen? You seemed so happy together the other night at the bar." said

Brandy gently, all the while feeling annoyed at having to deal yet again with Tray.

Tray looked down at his feet and said, "Well, to be honest, as soon as you left." He shifted from foot to foot nervously. "I despise that kind of controlling woman," he added, "so I ended it."

"Tray, you are a nice guy, I am sure there is a wonderful woman just around the corner for you. However, it is not me. We had our try at making us work, it just didn't. So, let's leave well enough alone and each go our separate ways. I will always care about you, you know this, just not in that capacity." Brandy tried to sound firm but gentle, as Tray walked away, feigning sadness for her benefit, as he was quite sure she was still watching him.

That day was finally over, thank heavens! It had not gone as she had expected, but in some ways it had actually gone better. Now she would have some closure in this matter.

She waited by the front door of *The Times* for Lucy to finish up. She had already given her number to Stuart and he planned to call in a bit to iron out the details of that evening's date. She tried to feel excited about it, tried hard to, but it just didn't stir up any excitement in her. Stuart felt more like a friend. Still, it was a night out and she did not mind the company.

Finally, Lucy arrived; "So sorry Hun, so sorry. I had so much to do there in the last few minutes. I'm ready now though. Oh, you got chocolates? And you got a card, and a..., is that a rose? Ewww, did you drop it?"

Together the two girls walked to Brandy's car. On the walk over, they discussed work and where she had gotten the gifts. But, once in the car, both girls were quiet, deep in thought about the day and their upcoming evenings.

Lucy planned to go to a party one of the girls from the diner was throwing. She invited Brandy along too if she wanted to go. Brandy may have gone under other circumstances, but not this time. Tonight she had a date of her own.

Just as they pulled into the parking space of their apartment, the car died. It must have known they were home. Just lovely, thought Brandy. She knew at that moment that she was definitely selling this car. It would be much cheaper to do without a car anyway, and just use the public transportation to get wherever she was going. Yes, it was crowded on public transportation, but it did its job, it got her to her destination and that's all she cared about.

3

Close Only Counts
in Horseshoes

Having called a mechanic, she called Stuart to tell him the bad news about her car. True to form, he said it would not be a problem. He recommended she ride over with the tow truck to the repair shop, where he could pick her up and continue on to their dinner plans. Her car had been having major issues with starting and running, having described the specifics to the repair shop, they told her that it was probably the battery.

She felt like it was probably more than that, a really good charge still didn't last as long as it should have. She would have put off having it repaired at all, except she would need to have it up and running if she was going to try to sell it. Her mind shifted back to thoughts of Stuart. Brandy truly needed someone like Stuart in her life. Someone thoughtful on whom she could rely, a steady man. A man who didn't tell her lies. One that she could count on when times were tough. She deserved a man that would treat her well, and who was a hardworking man. Was that too much to ask?

For their date, Stuart had taken her to a karaoke bar. They had ordered drinks, and both got up to sing. Brandy sang her standby- "The Gambler" by Kenny Rogers. It was a song with no high notes and nothing super low either. With her alto voice, she actually sounded pretty good singing it.

Then it was Stuart's turn. He really had a very nice singing voice. He sang Sam Smith's Stay With Me. That happened to be her favorite song at the moment. He had some nice rich tones to his voice, and sounded sexy when he sang. Not at all like the "work Stuart" she knew, which was a good thing.

She was having a great time. Maybe it was the Long Island Iced Teas she was sipping that were causing these emotions, but she found herself noticing Stuart's butt a good deal of the time. He was wearing some black jeans that seemed to be just the right amount of tight on him.

Gee, it had been a minute since she had been with a man. She forgot what she had been living without. But she was pretty sure Stuart was actually cute and a good catch. He came very close to what she had in mind for a proper mate, and it wasn't just the time she had spent without a man, the alcohol consumed, or the fact that she was horny.

Meanwhile, Lucy was having a blast at her friend's party. At least, that was what Brandy inferred from her roommate's happy, slurred speech over the phone when Lucy called her halfway through the evening. There had been music playing in the background through most of the phone call. Good, thought Brandy. She deserves to have a nice time.

It was sometime after midnight before Stuart dropped Brandy back off at the apartment. She saw a light on in the apartment window and knew that Lucy was already home. Guess that made sense, the party had been at the diner and that wasn't far away.

She knew that Lucy may have invited someone over, and he could be there right now even. She didn't want to walk in on them unannounced, plus Lucy deserved some privacy. She and Stuart stayed in his car and talked. Brandy had had such a nice evening. If Lucy had not been home, she likely would have invited Stuart up for coffee, coffee and maybe some dessert.

Lucy must have had quite the night as well. Lucy ended up going to work an hour late that next morning, but used Brandy's dead car as the excuse.

A potential buyer was supposed to be coming to see the car and test drive it the very next day. Thankfully, she had a laptop computer to work from when she was not at the office.

She was surprised to see Lucy arrive home early at 2pm. "Not dooo closed do me please, I have da flu." Lucy struggled to say through a tissue covered stuffy nose. "I dew dis was more dan justa a-a-achoo uh hangover." She sneezed while she ended it.

Well, this was way more than three bad things, they were on some kind of a spree of bad. They needed to do something to break this curse and fast. She couldn't afford any more car repairs. She also had no more long-term boyfriends to dump her, no more beloved dogs to lose, and she didn't wanna even think of losing her brand new job, she just loved it.

The Times was comprised of small offices, and like other small offices, news traveled fast. Brandy had heard a rumor that Tray had learned of her and Stuart's dating, and had not taken the news well. Not only was he not happy about it, he intended to do something nasty and vindictive, like turn them in to HR. As it worked out, he would not need to.

Rebecca Jones, the HR Generalist entered Stuart's office to consult with him on a matter involving one of the columns. She would normally have knocked, but the door was slightly ajar. As she walked in, Rebecca was surprised to find Stuart and his secretary Shelly locked in a passionate kiss. Stuart was seated at his desk and Shelly stood behind him. They had turned to conform to the angles needed to affect the embrace. They immediately stopped and righted themselves when she entered.

This did little good at that point. A meeting with Human Resources was now inevitable.

When the Reps called Brandy and Stuart down to the HR office for the "meeting," she thought she knew why, but she had never been more wrong.

She was told by Stuart that he had discussed their dating with Human Resources already and had received the "okay." Unfortunately, that was just not so. In fact, this meeting had little to do with Brandy at all.

In Human Resources, she sat awkwardly across from Stuart. Had there been a way to do so silently, she would have asked him about everything, but as it was she was too fearful that everything they now said was being recorded. She had heard stories.

Also, the look on Stuart's face told her all she needed to know, or at least she thought it had, until Shelly showed up. She chose a seat one over from Stuart's.

That seemed odd to Brandy as there were many other available seats she could have taken. Most of the ones by Brandy were empty for instance.

Then, finally, in walked some of the Human Resource employees. "Thank you all for coming here today." They began. "We hope this will not take up too much of your time. It seems that some rumors have been going around the office. They have reached us and when that happens we must take action. In light of what just took place upstairs today, well, we felt it best to get to the bottom of things quickly."

Brandy was at a loss. What had just happened upstairs today? She had not even seen Stuart all morning, or Shelly for that matter. Nor had she had any dealings with the staff from HR today, what were they talking about? And why was Shelly here?

Rebecca of Human Resources spoke next. "Stuart, would you please confirm that not long ago you came to us here in Human Resources and sought permission to date Ms. Brandy Goshen. Is this correct?"

"Yes." Stuart replied. He was looking very pale and like he may lose his lunch at any moment.

Rebecca continued; "And, despite that being against company policy, we made an exception in your case to do so, did we not? But then this morning I walked into your office to a rather unusual situation, just prior to your coming down here. Care to explain?"

"Yes, please do," thought Brandy, "because I have no idea what's going on."

"Yes, well," Stuart began "Shelly, Uh, Ms. Smith and I were going over some forms for a meeting, and well...I guess one thing led to another and when she leaned over my shoulder that way, well... I'm sorry. Normally I would never have allowed something like this to occur! We only shared one kiss, that's all."

"Is that what happened Ms. Smith?" Rebecca asked, "Or please, give us your version."

"I am sorry too, yes, we did kiss, but I wasn't leaning over Stuart to make a pass at him. I really was just trying to read the forms that were on his desk."

"Who made the first move? Who made the advances?" demanded Tom, the Senior Human Resources Manager. Stuart spoke up, taking the blame. "It was my doing, Tom," he admitted. "I was the one to pull her to me and kiss her." He turned to Shelly, who was sitting very still. "I'm sorry Ms. Smith."

Brandy was hurt, but she couldn't help feeling sorry for the offenders. "I have an idea," she said quietly. "Just let these two date. You'd already given your permission for him and me to date, so what is the difference? We proved to be mostly just friends anyway. Stuart is a great guy, and I like Ms. Smith too. But I am not looking to get anyone in trouble here."

"Well, that is very kind of you, Ms. Goshen. But we have policies in place and we must follow them regardless of what you may excuse." Tom said.

"Yes, it's a bit more complicated than that I'm afraid," said Jack Klondike. "Stuart, you and I have known each other for how many years now? It's been quite a while," he said, answering his own question. "In that time, have I ever not told it to you straight? Told you just exactly what was on my mind?"

"No, Jack, you've always been honest with me," Stuart admitted.

Tom started right back up as soon as Jack drew breath. "This is a place of business, so I am not going to permit myself to use the kind of language I would like to with you. But goddammit son, you disappoint me here. I know you know how to behave socially and ethically in a place of business."

Now at this point, Tom, who was a mammoth of a man, was right up in the face of Stuart. Brandy was intimidated by him, and she was nowhere near him. Tom evidently was not done speaking.

"We are decent friends and certainly we have known each other far too long for me to have to be calling you down here like this. If there is any, and I mean any cause for a problem of this nature for you in the future, you call me first, you hear, call me right away!

"So here it is," he continued. "We are not going to terminate either one of you, as this is a first offense for each of you, but we are going to have to suspend pay to each of you, for two weeks. I am sorry, I know it may sound harsh, but you can't fart in this office without the whole company knowing in a matter of minutes, it's such a tight knit work space. We must set an example or we would have this kind of thing happening all over the building."

Finally, that wretched day was over. Brandy was back home. She filled the tea kettle, put it on to boil, and went to sit at her desk. She still had to put some pictures in for an article on homeless pets and how to adopt them. There was going to be an adoption event in the park near their flat over the upcoming weekend, and she and Lucy had spoken of perhaps getting a dog for protection. Her mom had said it would make her feel a whole lot better if they did.

Lucy, still feeling under the weather, had chicken noodle soup for dinner, as she was not up for solid food. Brandy made leftover pizza and soda and plopped down to finish up her work. She got it done just as the clock struck 8pm. As much as had happened, they were just lucky to have jobs and a working car by the day's end.

The next morning, as they were about to head to the office, the car would not start again. "How is this possible?" She demanded of her car. "You have a new battery and a new alternator." She was reasoning with her car at this point. Well, she knew Lucy was used to not having a car, so she figured they would just walk to work and she would call the tow truck when they got back home. This very well may be the last they see of this car. It was going up for sell tomorrow.

4

Lucy's Accident

Walking in to work from the bus stop, the girls got a bit separated. Brandy was almost speed walking, but Lucy was trailing behind. She was talking on her cell phone and was not paying a great deal of attention to where she was going.

That quick, a giant commercial lorrie struck her. "Oh my God, Lucy, are you alright?" Brandy knew she wasn't, but the question came out anyway.

Brandy wasted no time calling 999. An ambulance arrived there straight away. Lucy was unconscious, appeared to have several broken bones and there was blood everywhere. Brandy wondered how her friend's life could change so quickly.

The ambulance pulled up and two paramedics who seemed to be reenacting a scene from a slapstick routine came fumbling out. Somehow, they managed to get Lucy on the stretcher and strapped in, but then one of the paramedics knocked the whole gurney over on its side due to sheer carelessness.

"Good God!" exclaimed Brandy, "What in the hell are you doing?

"You need to be much more careful with her. She is bleeding for Christ's sake!" she shouted at the careless paramedic.

"Why the hell are you even here lady?" he screamed back. "Were you driving the truck that hit her? You were weren't ya?" He asked in a very accusatory way, not allowing time for a response.

"God no! I was not, I was on foot, and so was she. I was looking the other way, but evidently she was not watching where she was stepping and went off the curbside, that must have been when the lorry hit her," cried Brandy.

Brandy would definitely be sharing their ineptness with their company, and perhaps a lawyer as well.

"No," contradicted a man on the sidewalk, "the lorry delivering ran up on the curb here and hit her!" Another eyewitness approached the officials and added, "I saw the whole thing!"

"Oh, were you an eyewitness to the accident?" asked the arriving police officer.

"Was indeed, saw the whole thing myself," said the same guy. "Name's Ian, Ian Burton." Ian said, directing his response to the officer.

"Thank you sir, we will need to ask you a few more questions. If you don't mind stepping over here to the side a minute," the officer said to Ian.

Brandy rode along with Lucy in the ambulance and used that time to call several of Lucy's contacts, one call each to her family, her job, and her friends at the diner. Brandy would later call her own people to let them know what was going on.

The lorry driver had stopped, thank heavens. He said he had not seen her at all, and then suddenly saw her in front of him. He said she had stepped off the curb and right into his line of vision, and that he had tried to avoid hitting her, but could not.

The witness, Ian, told a totally different story. One that implicated the lorry driver, stating that he had jumped the curb with his vehicle. Brandy also called Stuart. They were still close as friends, despite all else that had gone down. Good ol' Stuart. He would help, he would know what to do. She was glad they had kept their friendship intact. Stuart told her not to worry, that he was on his way out to the hospital, and that he had a lawyer friend who could expedite matters for Lucy too.

"Okay, okay," Brandy kept repeating to herself, as she paced the floor in the hospital waiting room. "Okay, let me think here. Called the office and let them know, called Lucy's family and let them know, called Lucy's friends at the diner and let them know." She was silently ticking off the mental to-do list in her head.

Everyone had been called; all of Lucy's people and even Brandy's people. There really wasn't anything else she could do from the hospital, but she felt like she ought to be doing something.

There was not much news to tell at first, other than that she had "broken several bones in her body." That was no great shock to hear from the doctors. Brandy was no medical professional but could have diagnosed that much on her own.

When Stuart finally arrived at the hospital, Brandy was just about beside herself with worry. She didn't know if she could handle doing all of this by herself. Someone would surely have to be by Lucy's side constantly, but that just couldn't be her. She had a job to do already, and God love her, but it didn't directly involve taking care of Lucy. If Lucy's family didn't step in, she would need to contact someone to help full time with Lucy, at least at first. There was just so much to be arranged.

Stuart put his arm around Brandy's shoulders, she pulled away for a moment, but when she saw the genuine care on his face, she let him hug her.

"Hey, Brandy, I am here Hun, it's all going to work out, you'll see. She has lots of family, and even more friends. The company is here too, and we'll all help out... I am here too...if that at all matters anymore to you." He added almost as an afterthought. Brandy wasn't at all sure what to think of that. But she was grateful for his being there now.

They would hear the term "distracted walker" a great deal over the next few weeks to months, it would likely be the lorry driver's only defense. Brandy had remembered doing an article on that topic recently.

"Okay, okay," Brandy began again, she needed to keep herself busy doing something. She couldn't just sit there and do nothing while Lucy lay clinging to life. She began to pace the floor once again. Stuart had just left, he had stayed as long as he could, but did have work he needed to get done that day. The news didn't wait for you after all.

Just then, her cell rang. It was Lucy's older brother, Greg.

"Oh my God Brandy, thank goodness you're there. What happened?" Brandy was used to speaking to Greg on the phone, she typically did so each time he called the apartment to speak to Lucy. Today, she told Greg all she knew about the accident, and about Lucy's health.

5

Is Anyone Writing This Down?

It occurred to Brandy that her life over the last few months was more like a made-for-television movie. This amount of drama was surely more than should be endured by any one person in such a short period of time. Luckily Lucy's family was coming into town to see her and to help. Any help at this point would be welcomed.

Brandy had only done the things that involved phone calls, and had not even tried leaving the hospital since getting there this morning. Lucy was still in critical condition, and the doctors predicted she was likely to be in the same state for at least a few days.

They had also told Brandy that as she was not a relative, she would not be kept up on the details of Lucy's recovery without something in writing. She would speak to the family about that right away, especially if she was expected to know or do anything in their absence.

Her mind went to Stuart, he seemed to still care for her greatly, but Brandy knew better than to give her heart fully to any man anymore. She had been deeply hurt one too many times. And anyway, she needed a man who could keep his mind on her and her alone for longer than sixty seconds. Well, that was how long it felt anyhow.

Just then, interrupting her thoughts was the ring of her cell phone. Whose number was this? She didn't recognize it. Her caller ID read Paris as the city of origin. Probably Lucy's family again, she thought. Sure enough, it was Greg calling from his cellphone.

"Hey Greg. Yes, she is resting comfortably. God, it was just horrific. There is a witness who says Lucy was not at fault, Stuart has a good lawyer on it as we speak, and there's a witness that says the lorry driver jumped the curb. Of course he is denying any responsibility for anything, according to him she stepped off the curb right in front of him."

Brandy had never actually met Greg, or most of Lucy's family for that matter. All she knew was that they lived in France but were originally living in London. And that Lucy had three other siblings - two brothers and a sister. Greg was the eldest, Lucy the youngest of the four.

Brandy and Greg had a very long phone conversation there in the hospital waiting room. Over the course of the conversation, Greg explained that he and Lucy were especially close, despite their birth order. They had very similar mannerisms and personalities and got along well. They had been each other's confidantes for most of Lucy's teenage years, and this is what had caused such a tight bond between them.

Greg seemed very kind and also very concerned about Lucy. He added that he and his family were all traveling to London together by plane and should arrive at the London City Airport in just a few hours, as the flight was scheduled to leave shortly. They were coming in tonight.

Dear God, tonight? She had to do a thousand things to prepare. The flight was due in around 6:00 PM, the time now was about 3:00 PM. She knew it took about an hour and a half or so to get from Paris to London by plane, but you had to factor in time for disembarking and baggage claim.

Brandy asked Greg if anyone was already planning on picking them up and bringing them to Lucy's house. Greg said he was renting a car upon arrival and planned to just drive in.

"Oh, that's right, you and Lucy share the apartment now. Is it going to be a problem for us to stay there? Cause, I mean, we could just rent a hotel room."

"No, it's no problem. With Lucy in the hospital, the whole place will be empty except me, and I pretty much stay in my room doing my computer work most of the day," said Brandy. "So, you all will basically have the run of the place."

"The rest of the family will only be staying for a night or two. They will then be returning to Paris, as long as Lucy is in stable condition," added Greg. "I plan to stay on longer, as I can do my work from my laptop anywhere, but I can always go to a hotel once they leave."

Brandy was about to counter that with an offer of her going, or no one going, but another flight being called over the airport intercom came on in French. "Oh, hey Brandy, that was the announcement for our flight, gotta go. See you soon," said Greg, ending the call.

Okay, she thought, well, I need to blow up air mattresses and make up beds, and ready the whole place for company. Plus get food in, and Lord only knows what all else.

Thankfully, her car had not sold yet. She would need it, after all. In fact, she had never even shown the car to the man who was to come out and test drive it that same day.

Brandy sighed, she should probably call him too and tell him she was sorry for standing him up, but that it was no longer for sale. Just one more thing on her to-do list.

6

I Had a Dream

Ever since she was a child, Brandy had been plagued with nightly anxiety attacks.

These nightmares had been a recurring problem, and although they would occasionally go away for a few months, they always resurfaced particularly in stressful times. For Brandy, these were such times.

Brandy had fallen asleep rather quickly, in comparison to other nights. But, once asleep, she slept fitfully. All of her insecurities worries and fears came rushing back to her. And although she had not seen it, Lucy's accident came to her mind as well.

All forms of scary thoughts filled her head and her dreams with their ugliness. They would often come back again the following day, but as anxiety, worry, or unfounded fear.

Thankfully, although she had one, it was a mild nightmare that evening. The next morning would bring visitors.

"Knock, knock, Greg? Brandy? We're here!" Janet yelled. Lucy's family had finally arrived at the apartment. Despite Lucy's condition, they tried to remain in good spirits.

"Hi, welcome, come on in! This is the little abode. I made up lots of places to sleep, hope they are all comfortable enough," added Brandy. "If you guys need anything that you don't have, just let me know. I have a ton of stuff, and you are all welcomed to any of it. Oh, and I ran out to the grocery store and brought in all the basics, but if you want me to pick up anything in particular, just write it on the list here."

Brandy pointed to the grocery list magnet that was on the front of her fridge. She loved that thing, it was so helpful. She loved all lists though, that was just how she was.

The Caldwell family would have arrived sooner, but they had stopped at the hospital first. This was fine, as it allowed Brandy time to ready things for their arrival. "How is Lucy today?" asked Brandy.

"Oh, she is in real good spirits, but then you know our Lucy, always one to put a positive spin on things." Janet replied.

"Any news from the doctors on how her recovery is going?" asked Brandy. "They won't tell me anything because I am not a relative."

"Yes, let's get that fixed while we are here today. We can fill out some paperwork that will allow you to at least know what is going on, and that way you can better keep us informed," Greg offered.

"The nurse seems to feel it won't be too long before she gets to come home. She will still need a nurse when she gets here though, of course. Don't worry Brandy, we will see to all that," said Janet kindly.

"Lucy will be fine Hun, she is one tough cookie," replied Bill, Lucy's dad. As Brandy and Janet set the dinner table and prepared something to eat, they talked about a plan of action for the next few months.

"Now, we want to help out in any way possible, just let us know Brandy. Whatever you think she is going to need for when she comes back here," Janet restated. "Oh, and has her job been involved in all of this?"

Brandy spent the next hour or so explaining all she had been learning about Lucy's recovery online. She went on to tell all she had done from a work-related perspective, which would allow Lucy to work from home while she recovered.

This would prove to be a godsend for Lucy, as her mobility would be almost non-existent, at least at first.

"God, you're great! Thank heavens you were here for Lucy in this terrible time of her life," said Greg. Bill spoke up and added, "What would we have done without you, Brandy?" This made Brandy blush a little. She was not used to having great looking men in her apartment, let alone ones who were gushing over her.

Brandy responded, "Well, it's not been all that difficult, I just made up some extra beds and bought food. Thank God my car had not sold. I would have had all those groceries to get home on the bus, even a taxi would have posed a few challenges, since I had to make a bank machine run, too."

Lucy's family had been in town for a week. They had only planned to stay for one or two days originally. It had gone by so quickly. Brandy would be sorry to see them go. They were a very sweet and close-knit family. It was apparent to her that they also loved Lucy a great deal. Her every need was met and they saw to it that her future needs would also be taken care of.

Brandy had even been compensated for all the time and effort she had put forth in caring for Lucy, though she had neither asked for nor expected such.

An icy rain fell again from the London sky. Brandy shivered just thinking of the walk from work to her car. It was running much better now, for no apparent reason.

One morning it had just decided to fix itself, she guessed. Maybe it realized it would be sold if it didn't shape up? She just didn't know. It was likely a temporary fix; problems like that tended to resurface.

The sky was very dark and Brandy felt cold and alone. Thank heavens she was not going home to an empty flat. Greg would be there. It was actually a warm and pleasant thought. She turned the key to her unit just as Greg opened the door. He must have been listening for her.

"Well, hey - an automatic door! How nice," she joked.

"Here, drink this. It's warm, but not too hot." Greg said while handing Brandy a cup.

"What is it?" she asked, holding the warm cup of unfamiliar smelling drink in both hands as she did.

"It's a Hot Toddy," said Greg, "but easy on the Toddy. I didn't know if you drank, but then, the alcohol *was* here." he grinned. "I know Lucy drinks though, so I figure it could be hers. She won't mind."

"I have heard of these, what's in them exactly?" wondered Brandy aloud.

"Well, they are a cure for whatever ails ya back where I come from. They have whiskey, water, sugar, and some spices. Plus I added a little bit of ginger ale. Hope you like it. It will help you keep the weather out of your lungs and outside. At least that is what my Scottish Grandma Caldwell used to say."

"And where in Scotland is that? I thought you all were from France?" asked Brandy, abruptly.

"Well, yes, we live in France now, and we do have French from mom's side, but we are also half Scottish, from Dad's side – hence, our sir name is Caldwell. That was dad's dad, and I am speaking of his mom."

"Oh, I see, and what were you going to say about the Hot Toddy, before I cut you off?" she laughed.

"It is thought to have originated in India, way back in the 1600-1800's by the East India Company, actually," he said. As he spoke, her eyes showed her amazement, and he began to crack a sly grin. All the while she looked at him admiringly.

He was pleased that his knowledge impressed her so greatly. She would find that his brain was chocked full of such facts, and many others, about anything and everything. He was incredibly knowledgeable about a great variety of topics. Brandy felt she could listen to him speak all day.

Brandy had tried to pass the time by playing Trivial Pursuit with him earlier in the week, back when his family was still there. She soon found him just impossible to beat. Sort of a walking set of encyclopedias, if he was really trying to play to win, and he was most of the time.

But then she had done something wrong. She had jokingly teased him by calling him a dunce.

She never would have called him that if she had been thinking, but she spoke before she thought. It was out of her mouth before she knew it. She had said it with all kindness and well meaning.

It was more of a passing thing, or a term of endearment really when she said it, but his feelings had been hurt nonetheless. She had been placed on a team with Greg, and on the opposing team were Janet and Bill.

She had been in the middle of a fiercely competitive round with Bill, and she was trying to play just a little badly so his dad would win for sure, but he truly didn't need the accommodation.

When it came time for her and Greg's turn, she had said something like, "Well, I will go ahead and answer that then, or my dunce can answer for me."

Without meaning a thing by it, and certainly not meaning that she felt he was inferior intellectually, he must have taken it that way. Something was different. There was something almost tangible in the air. Brandy had always had almost a sixth sense when it came to reading people, especially men, and something was not the same.

7

List Item # 9; Meet a Great Man, Check

There was definitely a discernible difference in the air between them for the rest of that day and that next morning.

She had cut him, and she had not meant to. It had taken only a few minutes and only a few words, but it was done. Now there was no way she could unsay it, but she knew she could not leave things like that. Surely he realized nothing could be further from the truth?

Brandy had been nothing but impressed by Greg and his brilliance ever since she had first spoken to him over the phone many months before. Since then, he had done so much research on Lucy and her condition. He knew just what she would need to go through, just what to do for her rehabilitation as well. He would prove to be instrumental in readying her room when she was ready to do so.

He also spoke so many different languages, had traveled so many places, and had seen things she had only ever dreamed of seeing. He had seen the seven wonders of the world, traveled extensively, and done so many amazing things that she may never get to do if she lived six lifetimes. On top of all that, he had an amazing vocabulary, was very well-read and well-educated, and was not a bit hard on the eyes with his great butt and his gorgeous smile.

Indeed, Greg, though not a perfect man, was a very well-rounded man and in more ways than one. This she found herself noticing on more than one occasion.

Yet, he still managed to have little to no conceit. In fact, at times he was even unsure of himself. A rarity among accomplished men, for certain. He truly was nothing like Tray had been from her previous relationship.

Brandy had no control over when her nightmares occurred. At night, on any night, it could happen. It was a Friday night, and it was one such night. It was about two or three in the morning when Brandy awoke with a start due to one of her dreams. Thankfully, there was someone else in the house now. This seemed to comfort her from the feeling of terror that overtook her in moments like these.

Greg was in on the couch asleep. She tried her best not to wake him as she went for her glass of milk. She would have done without it all together, but it kept her from an upset stomach when she took her anti-anxiety pill. Her general practitioner had prescribed them for her back in the States, and she had just gotten them refilled before her move.

There was a bit of a glow from the TV still being on. She could see her way enough to walk through the kitchen, but once there, she was in the dark. If she could just get the door to the fridge open, it would be enough light to see to get the milk. Still feeling the buzz she was always left with after a night of her bad dreams, she opened the cabinet and removed a glass.

With glass in hand, she opened the door of the refrigerator and took out the milk. She was just about to pour herself a glass when Greg entered.

"Brandy, is everything alright?" he asked. He had been aware of her nightmares from the last time she had one, but that had been mild, unlike this episode. She was still trembling. He noticed her trembles and assumed she was chilly. Grabbing a sweater from the back of the chair in the nearby dining room, he draped her in it. It did seem to help her somehow. Or maybe it was just the human interaction.

Greg was just that thoughtful. Who else would have done that? Who else would even have thought to have done so? None of the other guys she had dated, or lived with, or even been married to, for that matter.

And over time, she had just steeled herself to being the one who was thoughtful in the relationship. She had learned to live without the return. It seemed her lot in life. But fortunately, she enjoyed caring for the needs of others. Making them happy felt good to her. It's who she was.

"Brandy, why don't you come in here and sit down a minute? I can get that for you," offered Greg. He led her to the living room sofa and sat her down, covering her with a throw to keep her warm. "Instead of having cold milk, would you like me to make up some special Hot Toddies again?" Greg offered.

"I would normally say yes, but as I just took an anti-anxiety pill, and I'm not supposed to have any alcohol with it," said Brandy, almost wishing she had not taken the stupid thing that now was going to interfere with her accepting anything special from Greg.

He poured himself a cup of orange juice and sat next to her on the couch. He pulled the throw over his lap too, and grabbed the remote control. With his arm up on the back of the couch, it made for an easy and warm nook in which to snuggle. She did so. They had not dated long enough, nor had they been together often enough, to create a close bond physically yet, but this was a start.

"What's on?" Brandy asked.

"No clue. I hope NCIS or something good. I love that show, and all crime solving shows."

Brandy did too. It was just one of the many things they would find they had in common.

"Suspense in movies is an awesome thing, don't you think?" asked Greg.

"Sometimes, unless my own life has enough in it already," answered Brandy honestly.

They began to scroll through the channels to see what was on. They said the names of the shows out loud as the channels went past; *Losing Graces, Trading Places, Winning Cases, Empty Places.* There was a definite theme trending in naming shows, and they were becoming very aware of this only now.

It all began to look alike, until Greg exclaimed, "There! Finally, a crime show. Let's watch this."

Oh, it proved to contain crime alright. But it was no crime solving show, it was a horror film. Brandy didn't usually watch those, especially when she had just had a nightmare. In fact, she rarely ever watched those anymore. But, here in Greg's arms she felt different...safe, like she could watch this and still be okay. Another positive change in her, and she liked it.

She must have fallen asleep there. She didn't remember seeing the ending to the show, only that she woke up to a beautiful face, Greg's, sitting next to her on the couch. He was groggy and had some serious stubble going on, but he was a wonderful sight to her. She snuggled in closer.

"Well good morning." said Greg.

"Good morning, did I fall asleep here? I'm sorry. You must have frozen, and not have gotten any sleep trying to share the couch and one cover with me," apologized Brandy.

"No, I didn't sleep, I watched you sleep. I was fine here. I was plenty warm."

"Oh, Greg, I'm sorry. You should have woken me up, instead of letting me sleep on your arm that way. It is going to hurt you today."

"Are you hungry?" he asked, changing the subject. It always seemed to him that she was apologizing for or preaching and correcting something. He didn't like that, but it was a little thing. She cared so much; that was her motive.

She was actually aware of it in herself too, and had made great strides to correct it. She really didn't mean to come off like that. She knew he was no child, she just cared so much. About people in general, yes, but about him in particular, definitely.

"I'm a little bit hungry, but here, let me get up and make us some breakfast. What would you like Sir Greg?" Brandy asked.

"Well, that depends on what's on the menu," he answered, smiling. It was a leading question. He was softly flirting with her, and she knew it, but she didn't want to stop him. She was enjoying it, and him.

She could see how nice having him around all the time would be.

She tried not to notice, tried not to look either, but she just had to. The man was well endowed. It was first thing in the morning, and on a morning after a night of holding a pretty woman in his arms and not doing anything about it. It was bound to effect some changes on the male body.

"*Have mercy!*" thought Brandy. "*Dear Lord, this man is blessed in so many, many ways.*" She again tried not to make an issue out of it. After all, they weren't ready to sleep together. That was a step too far this early on in the relationship, but God, the thoughts that went through her mind just then. She drew a deep breath in and held it. Slowly she released it and composed herself.

"Get it together here Brandy, get it together," she warned herself.

"So, let me cook then, and you take the morning off. You have been cooking the whole time my family was here. My turn to wait on you," said Greg. "Come, sit, I will serve you ma 'lady." He added, as he pulled out a dining room chair, ushering her to take a seat.

"And, just what do you know how to make, sir?" she asked. She was unaccustomed to anyone making her breakfast, or any meal for that matter.

"Don't you trust me? It is a surprise," he replied.

She was only slightly uncomfortable with him taking over, a real upgrade from her usual OCD ways. Normally it would have driven her crazy to have someone come in and take over her kitchen, but that didn't seem to bother her nearly so much today. She relinquished all kitchen rights to him, at least for the morning.

He made French toast, egg-batter dipped, with scrambled eggs on the side. She would not normally eat this full of a breakfast, it was way too many calories for her, but no way was she going to complain. She just had smaller portions, savoring each bite. Was there anything this man could not do?

Everything Brandy did was from a list she had made up, whether it was the food she bought, the chores she did, or the books she read, they had all been listed. And of course her life goals.

Her morning had been going so well. She no sooner had thought *that* than the doorbell rang. It was Tray. *What in the hell was he doing here?* She wondered. She was secretly seething that he had the nerve to show up at her door at all, but she didn't say as much.

"Tray? What are you doing here?" Brandy asked puzzled, but keeping her tone in check. She was trying her best to be polite. His visit was totally unexpected, and unwelcome, but she would be civil. He had no response, so she went on to speak.

"Well, it's raining cats and dogs out there. Step in. Would you like a cup of coffee?"

"I'd like a cup of whatever you're serving baby." Tray replied, speech slurred.

"Look Tray, I am just being nice, I know it's cold and damp out there. Do you want the goddamned coffee or don't you?" demanded Brandy, in a much more testy manner than even she intended. She couldn't help it, he was interrupting her wonderful morning with Greg.

"Hey, sweet stuff, don't be so cross with me. I'm your Tray, remember?" He slid up against her. "Remember baby?" he repeated, "I can make you feel real good. You won't even remember anyone new."

Brandy struggled to push him away. She despised him, especially when he was not under his own control. Tray grabbed up Brandy before she could even react. He had obviously been drinking or something, and was just totally not himself. He was about to overpower her and make her lay back on the couch, when Greg heard the commotion. He ran into the room, charging at Tray as he did. The two had very little words before the punches started to fly. Brandy was stunned.

"Stop it! Stop this right now!" she screamed, but no one heard her. The fighting continued. Tray had hit first, but that didn't mean Greg was going to do nothing about it. Greg swung a hard right hook and caught the chin of Tray in an undercut. Tray went about a foot or two off the ground and landed on the coffee table, smashing it to the floor. Blood was everywhere. Tray had gotten a few good punches in himself - one to Greg's eye, a second to his mouth. It appeared both men would need stitches, or at least first aid. Brandy wanted to call the police, but Greg insisted that it was no big deal, as long as Tray left peacefully. Tray called someone to come and pick him up, so there were no worries there. What an asshole. Boy, was she glad she didn't stay with him.

Some divorces or breakups were unnecessary perhaps, but some were definitely called for. Hers was the latter. She had never told another living soul, but she had been pregnant at the time he and she were together. She lost that child, but felt that that may have been in God's plan to spare that child any more sorrow.

Greg was nothing like Tray, though. He was kind, thoughtful, and even looked out for his enemies best interests. Who does that? And most of all, he was humble. That's what appealed to Brandy the most about him.

She had met several other accomplished and successful men in her past, but the one thing they all seemed to have in common was their high level of conceit. Nothing turned her away faster.

So far, she was very impressed by Greg. "Just who is this man I've had sleeping in my home?" He intrigued her. She just may need to devote some serious time toward getting to know him better. *That* was definitely going on the top of her to-do list.

Brandy went outside for her morning run. Greg would normally go with her, but said he had an urgent call he needed to make, so he stayed in. Once Brandy was outside,

Greg got on the phone. He placed a call to America. It was to the home of his ex-wife. He called there regularly. He wanted to speak to his son and his daughter. Jonah and Jennifer were his whole world. He tried to catch up on their school, their friends, their accomplishments, everything he could over the phone. With only having shared custody, it would be the holidays before he would have the chance to see them.

8

Lucy Comes Home

It was a Thursday when the call came to Brandy that Lucy was being released. She (and Lucy's family of course) could not have been happier. She and Greg had just been out to visit Lucy the day before, and her nurse had said they were close to letting her go home, so they had worked together all that evening on Lucy's room.

While she was working at her computer, Greg had driven Brandy's car to go to the store to shop for supplies. Brandy had gone in to work a few times for this or that, but had for the most part, been working from home. Greg had been staying in their apartment all this time.

They would need to go pick up Lucy shortly. She was not back to normal, not by a long shot, but in time, with physical rehab, rest, and lots of care, she eventually would recover.

It had been close to a month since Lucy's accident. She had settled nicely back into her own room at home. A nurse came and checked in on her each day, as well as handled her physical therapy.

Brandy tried to pay as much attention to what she did as she could, so that when the nurse no longer came, she would still be able to assist Lucy herself. Brandy went over and mentally checked off the items on her to-do list for the day. The food was in the house, Lucy had done her therapy for the day, and her nurse had aided her in the shower. Brandy had just finished the article she was working on and was now adding the stock photos to it.

That is when Greg brought in a tray of food. First, he had taken one in to Lucy, but now he had brought one for Brandy as well. God, this was a considerate man. She felt like she was finally getting to know Greg, the real Greg. The one who could fart in front of her and merely laugh it off.

She didn't know him all that well yet, but if he kept this up, it would not be for a lack of her trying. She was constantly impressed by all he said and did. Was he acting this way on purpose just to impress her? Well, if he was, he was succeeding.

She decided to speak with Lucy about him when he next left the house. She was not ready to admit it, but perhaps she had the tiniest crush on him. She would wait and bide her time on that.

She did have questions, like was he seeing someone else? Oh my God! Was he married? She didn't even think to concern herself with that one! But she didn't think so, though. Was he a dad with kids? (Having not been around when he had placed the call home to the US, she did not hear him speak to his children Jonah and Jennifer, or she would have been even more impressed. He would be a good one, if so. He was very patient when teaching or educating animals and other people's children. That was almost always a good ruler for being a great parent yourself. How did any of this play into her life? She did not know.

Still, if Lucy was any help at all, she soon would know. At least that was her plan anyway.

Lucy was craving Chinese food. Everything else was delivered there except Chinese. Greg volunteered to go pick it up from a nearby restaurant.

Excellent, that would give Brandy the alone time she needed with Lucy to ask her questions. She didn't want to overburden Lucy with anything. Emotionally, Lucy was not quite up to par just yet. An accident can take a lot from a person's psyche, healing it would require a bit more time.

Lucy however could not have been more interested in that particular topic. In fact, she seemed to have anticipated Brandy asking her all kinds of things about Greg. Evidently, Greg had already asked Lucy his own questions regarding Brandy.

"Come in here and close that door. I want to know everything, I want to hear it all, now spill!" demanded Lucy, excitedly. "What's going on?"

So now it was official, she and Lucy were on the same level. She and Lucy were just two young girlfriends whispering about the romantic interest one had in a boy. They were almost giddy. It would have been silly if they could have seen what they looked like on the outside.

"Oh my God, Brandy. You two would be so perfect together. Have you kissed? Did he tell you anything about his feelings? Talk woman, fill me in, I feel like I have been so out of the loop lately." Actually, Lucy was not as out of the loop as she had claimed. She had just received the scoop from her earlier interrogation of Greg, but this way, she would have both sides of the story.

Brandy began to fill Lucy in on well, nothing. Nothing had really happened yet. She just explained her feelings. She did have questions though. Those same questions. So she asked them of Lucy.

Lucy was more than forthcoming with the answers, too. She really liked Brandy and was rooting for them to get together. That was quite a compliment, too, as Greg was Lucy's favorite brother.

In short, she had determined that yes, Greg had been prior married. Yes, he had a couple kids who resided in America with Greg's ex-wife. No, he was not currently seeing anyone. Yes, he had asked several questions about Brandy and had told Lucy he thought she was a very attractive and intelligent woman, and intriguing as well.

If those were his exact words or not, she did not know. But she felt that very same way about him too. Now she really did plan to get to know this man better.

She would have to speak with him sooner or later, and she had no idea how that was going to happen. He was scheduled to return to France in just a few days.

From what she had picked up on herself, as well as gotten from Lucy, Greg was a very sensitive man. No wonder it had not taken much to hurt him the way she had, but he seemed to have healed from that well enough.

In the future, Brandy would have to show greater care when dealing with Greg. She would have to not be so careless with her speech. She was not used to choosing her words carefully. In fact, she was very used to saying whatever came to her mind and letting the chips (or words) fall where they may.

Now that she understood this about him, she wanted to correct it in herself. This was a positive sign of self-growth. (She knew this from a self-help book she was reading. It was the current book from Morning Talk Show Diva Optra's must read book list, which she kept up with religiously.)

It also meant good things as far as having a healthy relationship of any kind with anyone. You had to be willing to conform at least a little in areas of your life where you came up short.

Greg finally arrived with the Chinese. "About time, we are starving in here!" yelled Lucy from her bed. She was smiling while she said it. Greg knew she was not really upset at all.

"Sorry, sis," he hollered back. "Between the traffic, and the line I had to wait in at the restaurant, it was ridiculous. They didn't have any more shrimp egg rolls, so I got you a pork one, is that okay?"

"I...guess..." dragged out Lucy, disappointedly, as if she were making the biggest sacrifice in the universe. She was just playing of course; brother and sister banter. It went back and forth like that on a regular basis, and they did that with almost everything. Brandy was almost envious that she had not grown up with a big brother like Greg.

Normally, they would have all eaten together at the table as a group. The Caldwell family was sticklers for this type of thing, and with good reason. It did promote conversation and draw families closer together.

But Lucy, although doing very well in her slow recovery, had not yet reached the point of being able to sit up for long periods of time at a table, desk, or any hard based location. She did well to sit propped up in her bed to use her laptop, and she did so daily. This is what Brandy had worked out for her at *The Times*.

Days had passed, and Greg was due to go home to France that very next morning. Lucy would miss him. Surprisingly, so would Brandy.

Either she was unwilling or unable to accept this in her own mind, but she knew it was true. She hated that she had any area of her life where she needed a man for anything. To her this was a sign of weakness, a lack of self-reliance, a lack of independence. A definite deficit.

She could not bear the thought of him leaving though and not returning. What did that mean? Always analyzing both her own as well as others thoughts and actions was the norm for Brandy. Was she falling for this guy? Did she even know him well enough to do so? Was he a safe bet?

Brandy never put money out on anything that wasn't. But she had gotten to know Lucy pretty well, thought she was great, and the family seemed on the up and up. Everything did, which should have acted to reassure her, but it had the opposite effect. She was feeling ill.

9

The Airport Once More, and Step on It!

B randy would obviously have to be the one to take Greg to the airport. Lucy was up more and more now, but could not afford to risk a fall or other injury at this crucial stage of her recovery. She would just need to stay home, despite wanting to see Greg off.

She did spend most of the day with her brother the day before. They had spoken in private, outside of Brandy's earshot. Lucy got down to the nitty-gritty with him regarding Brandy. She asked him all the questions she and Brandy had discussed.

Lucy pressed, "So Greg, I have to ask you; how do you feel about Brandy? No saying she's a great girl or any of that bullshit, I mean how do you feel about her, for real, for real."

"Goddamn Lucy, feelin' better are we? Am I allowed to have any secrets from my family? Any private thoughts or personal feelings at all? Any inklings, or inclinations that I don't immediately run to you all and tell?" Greg was angry, but he did deserve some privacy in his life.

"Greg! It's not like that. I'm sorry, I really was just wanting to know because I care about both of you. Well,

I love you, and I think Brandy is a great girl too. I am rooting for you guys," added Lucy. "Please don't be upset with me. If it's none of my business just say so. I will shut up right now."

"You know I could never do that, Dingleberry," he joked. "I am way too close to you. I care too much about your opinion to just brush it under the rug. But I need you to understand that although we are close, and we are family, some matters are just personal and are off limits!"

"I am about to fall asleep," Lucy said. "Don't leave without saying goodbye to me first."

"Never!" said Greg with a silly smile. "But you rest now. I'll still be here when you wake up. I just checked it on my cell, the flight back to Paris is not leaving until this evening. I don't know why I was thinking it left earlier. I think I am going to go challenge someone to a game of darts!" He spoke loudly in a stage voice intentionally so Brandy could hear. He winked at Lucy as he said it.

He was not always the world's most vocally expressive man, but with all else he had going for him, who would care? In fact, it was not that he lacked the feelings, nor did he lack the chops to express them, he just at times was a bit unsure of himself. As a result, he chose to keep his thoughts to himself.

There were other times though that he was quite vocal with his opinions. Brandy almost felt he would be the perfect person for their "Auntie Agony" column. Plus he knew so much about every topic under the sun; where he had read it, even the page and paragraph for most of the topics he spoke on.

He also knew five or six languages. Not just how to say hello, good-bye, and Taxi, but knew them, could read, write, and speak them. This just amazed Brandy.

Greg knew that after almost two months of living there in that tiny apartment with her, and all those times he had called for Lucy but spoke first with Brandy. That he would have to face up to their mutual attraction sooner or later. It wasn't that he feared responsibility, it was merely that, despite his excellent vocabulary, he was at times at a loss for words when it came to being around Brandy. Their relationship may just be new and budding, but to him, it felt like it could go somewhere.

As for Brandy, she didn't want to have to rely so heavily on her God given powers of perception. She already had to do that just to get this far in her life. But she didn't want to have to use her "powers" for deciphering men. She didn't *want* to, but it just happened, automatically, and without much effort on her part.

She intuitively knew what most men were thinking, especially if she had gotten to know them well enough first. Also, it didn't seem to take her as long as most to read folks in general. It was just something that was always in her to be able to do. One thing different about her too, was that she accepted imperfection in others without judgment. Or, if they had wronged her, she would just forgive them straight out. It was a very unusual quality.

As night fell, it approached time for his flight to leave. She was not clear on why but she did not want him to go. It wasn't as though she had fallen madly in love with him or anything. "God no!" Brandy thought. But she did care whether or not he approved of her choices, especially on important things. She valued his opinion highly.

For some reason, she cared what he thought on a lot, on matters such as whether she should put in for a better position at work, or if she should try to take on a mortgage at this stage of her life.

Normally, this was the kind of thing that she would usually want to bounce off of a friend or family member first before she jumped right in and made a life changing decision. And that made sense, but why immediately did her mind bring her around to Greg?

"Because I value his opinion," she answered her own mind.

She was an intelligent woman, and it wasn't her first time at bat. She was moving up in her career on her own, thank you very much, but mostly that had been due to the several failed relationships she had been through.

If any of those had actually worked out or lasted, likely she would not be on her own to make such decisions now. Each had ended for a logical and legitimate reason, but had ended nonetheless.

That meant she had always needed to make major life decisions on her own. Never consulting with, or relying on the opinion of anyone else, least of all a man. She wasn't anti-male, at least she didn't consider herself to be. Brandy had been in love with several men before. Love was a funny thing, though.

There were men from her past that would likely always hold a special place in her heart. Men whom she still liked, but never would love, men she loved but no longer liked due to things she had since discovered about them, and so on. Not likely any different than any other woman on the planet.

However, her new found singleness had introduced her to a world where not only did her opinion matter, but it was the only one there was. She had grown to trust herself to make important decisions on her own. So, why then did she seek out Greg? God, she wished she knew!

At 7:30 PM, they had to leave the apartment to get to the airport on time. His flight left at 9:00 PM as it was.

Fortunately, he had already secured his ticket. He did have to go through security to be checked out. Things like that always took longer than you would think.

In the car on the way over to the airport, the two were alone together for the first time all day. Lucy had been with them back at the apartment, and before that Brandy had been working. Now, it was just them.

She wanted to find out the answer to more of her questions, but only if it made sense for her to ask them. She didn't want anything to seem forced or artificial. But before she could think of a way to broach the topic, he did it for her.

"So hey, Brandy, can we speak candidly here for a minute? I have been staying in your apartment for almost two months now, and I don't want you to think I was trying to take advantage of you or my sister financially, so here's an envelope, it may not cover all of my family's expenses, but it should help."

Oh, thought Brandy disappointedly. She didn't care about that. She wanted his words, not his money. "Okay," she said and shoved it sight unseen into her purse.

"I also want to thank you for caring for my little sis the way you have, and for going above and beyond what anyone would have who just met this crazy family so recently," he added.

This waiting was excruciating. Someone was going to have to start speaking and soon as they were almost to the building, and then he would be leaving the country. "I just wanted to add that it has been my greatest pleasure getting to know you and spending time with you over these last few months," said Greg. "I am sure you will have to come and visit us in France soon."

"I would like that," Brandy replied.

"I also wanted to add that I think you are a wonderfully delightful woman who knows her mind and who doesn't take any guff from anyone. I admire that a great deal," said Greg.

To add to that, I find myself very attracted to you and wondered if you felt any of these same things toward me? Thought Greg. But he didn't say those words aloud, he merely thought them.

In all honesty, Brandy had been very impressed by his knowledge on just about every subject known to man. But she also was not ready to express any of her feelings to him yet.

"I am rather long-winded, and I am afraid that if I begin to answer your questions now, it will run you late for your plane. I guess it's just meant for another day," she said sadly.

"Just let me off right here, I will drop off my bags, be scanned and call you from the plane once I am seated. Then we will continue to have this conversation," said Greg.

"Sounds like a plan," said Brandy.

Greg was so elated that she had not turned him down, he felt like he had never run so fast in his life. Bags in hand, he ran into the airport doors, unbeknownst to her, he did not board the plane after all, but went instead went to what appeared to be a car rental desk.

Once he was finished with some paperwork, he was handed the keys and told that the vehicle was just out front, he made a quick stop for a purchase at one of the stores in the airport, and then headed outside.

After he loaded his bags into the car and was settled in, he was free to call Brandy's cell. He put it on speaker phone. By this point, she was almost back to the apartment. She parked, but sat in the car anyway for privacy.

When her cell phone rang, she answered after the second ring. "Well hello, any trouble getting on?" She didn't know what else she was supposed to say, they had just spoken not more than 45 minutes ago.

"Hi," he added with a chuckle "Is Brandy there?" He was playing with her mind and she knew it, but she did not mind in the least. It was a cute and flirty way he had about him and she just ate it up.

"No, I am sorry, she has stepped away, May I take a message for her?" she asked, innocently.

"Yes, could you let her know to open that envelope she stuffed into her purse, it may have something interesting in it for her." He was smiling in his speech.

"Oh, I sure will, I sure will." She was now laughing as well. What could be in that envelope? She had assumed that it was money for expenses, and had not given it a second thought, just shoved it in her purse. He was a tricky one, this Greg. "Please also ask her to call me the minute she finishes reading it too, if you don't mind.

"Will do," she snickered, "and have a nice day." She got off the phone as quickly as she could.

10

Taken For a Ride

"*What in the hell could he have put in a flat envelope?*" she wondered. Still outside her building, just sitting in her car, Brandy felt a little juvenile at her excitement, but she opened her purse and took out the envelope.

At the time he had given it to her, she assumed it contained money for his stay. That is how he had presented it. Now she looked at that envelope, it was rather thick, but not lumpy, so as to contain anything bulky or off the wall, but still thick with papers.

Not having the nail file she kept in her pen cup for opening envelopes at work, she used her finger and slid it under the fold, promptly cutting her fingertip as she did. "Dammit!" she screamed to an empty and unsympathetic car. She put the painful digit into her mouth and continued to remove the contents of the envelope.

She pulled out two plane tickets to Italy, cash, and a folded sheet of paper. Of the three, the one that appealed to her the most was the folded paper, because it contained his words.

Brandy loved words, as a writer, she played with words all day. These were his words, and his words were now so important to Brandy in the same way that Greg had become so important to her life.

Words were not only how she made her living, but how she expressed herself. They carried people's thought, ideas, and dreams.

Then her cell rang. It was Stuart. "Hey Brandy, just checking in on you, how is everything going for you and for Lucy? How is she these days?" he asked.

"She is coming along nicely," replied Brandy. "Thanks for asking." Stuart really was a thoughtful guy. It was a shame, in some ways, that things went down as they had with Stuart, but she was none too upset that she was left with Greg. None at all. Stuart kept the conversation on the up and up the whole time, which she had to give him credit for.

Shelly had moved on to a better paying position, and therefore a new man. She had never intended to make Stuart her "forever." Shelly was all for what she could get from people. She used men as stepping stones to advance her career. That was not unusual, many people, both men and women did it. It happened more than Brandy cared to think about.

In earlier positions, she herself had been offered better pay or higher positions if she would just make herself available to certain men, in certain ways. She however, was not that type of woman. She had morals, standards, and scruples. She cared a little bit more than she needed to perhaps about those things, and she took quite a bit of teasing about it too, but that was how she was raised. And while money paid the bills, it did little to motivate her the way it did most persons. No wrong man was worth putting up with just for his money.

Still in the car, in the lot next to her building, she focused once more on the task at hand. The contents of the envelope. The paper was the first thing she looked at.

She opened the paper and began to read: "Take these tickets and the money too, the letter and map will show you what to do." That was rhyming, and it was in his beautiful penmanship, but it was not poetry, nor was it the words she had hoped to see.

Brandy realized that there was indeed a small hand drawn map still in the envelope, carefully she retrieved it.

"God he had such nice artistry and penmanship," Brandy thought to herself, and smiled as she did.

And the map looked as if it could have been professionally printed, except clearly closer examination would tell you that it was done in ink by a talented hand. This took some doing and some skill, Brandy thought. Lucy did mention he was very creative.

The directions had said to take all the other contents of the envelope and to follow the map. She would know what to do when she got there. "Got where?" She wondered aloud. The map directed her to go back into the apartment. This was kind of halfway between fun and frustrating, She wasn't sure if she was enjoying it or not.

Quickly she gathered up all her things and her purse, she took out her keys, sadly knowing she would have to let herself into her apartment today, and from now on. Once inside, she was greeted by another note leading her to another clue.

She smiled and thought: "I remember this game from my childhood." She giggled at the thought of Greg writing and placing all the clues around the apartment. He really was a clever man.

The second clue was hanging from the ceiling, how had she not seen it there before leaving the house? "Ohhh," she said. "I see! It is also connected to a book on the bookshelf which could be removed or replaced to allow the adjustment of slack in the string."

The second clue said: "Your exploration has just begun, your anticipation is on the run, look in the place you usually are, you will find me in a jar."

"*Well Good Lord!*" she giggled, "*I usually am in my office at the computer when I am home; I will look there first.*" Sure enough, under her desk chair was a mason jar with something in it; another note.

She pulled it out and it said:" You are doing quite well, but are not there yet. Hope your patience holds out. It will, I'll bet. You have patient eyes. Your next clue lays where you'd make French fries."

She hurried off to the kitchen to look in the skillet. Okay, this was just a little bit fun. In the skillet, tucked under the spatula was yet another note, it read: "One last note to help you find, what you seek and some peace of mind. Go to where you do your hair, you will find some presence there."

"Oh, he had spelled it wrong." She thought disappointedly, "He meant I would find some presents there. That is so unusual for Greg to misspell a word like that." But she went to her makeup desk anyway. Taped to the very corner of the mirror of her makeup desk was the tiniest note she had ever seen, and was penned in pristine script, it read: "Turn around and you will see...me."

Brandy spun around and could not believe her eyes. "How could you be here? I just dropped you at the airport. I am so confused. Didn't you need to get home? How in the heck did you get back here without me knowing or noticing?"

Greg had to laugh. He wanted to answer her, but he couldn't without chuckling. When he had calmed down from laughing at himself, he answered her.

"It was simple really," he replied. "Immediately after you dropped me off, I rented a car, came here, saw you sitting out in your car, came up here and set up the last of the notes, and I've just been sitting here waiting for you to follow out the instructions to get to this point. Oh, and Lucy was in on it the whole time."

"But I don't understand, don't you have to be back at work?" asked Brandy completely puzzled.

"I made a call to work and they have everything well under control without me. Mom is going to water my plants and feed my dog, and I do almost all of my work from my laptop anyway, so here I am. I couldn't leave with us right in the middle of such an important conversation, now could I?" He asked in such a tender way, it almost surprised Brandy. "Let me feed Lucy, and then how about you and I go out and get something to eat ourselves and we can continue our conversation right where it left off?" Greg asked.

"Yeah, okay, feed Lucy. Okay." said Brandy, her mind in a thousand places. She was still puzzling over how all that could have been done, and right under her nose too, evidently. She went off into Lucy's room and asked her what she would like to have for dinner. Lucy was in a mood to mess with Brandy too, and answered, "Just a sister- in-law." and then she cracked up laughing.

"Ha ha...very funny, you two are just a riot today, and I understand you were in on all of this too?" Brandy shook her head. Guess you both like practical jokes then huh? Well, okay, I will keep that in mind. You may be sorry though."

She turned around and Greg had the food tray for Lucy. Once she was given her tray, Brandy and Greg left. "So, where do you want to eat, madam?" asked Greg.

"Will it be real food, or a will it make my teeth and tongue turn black?" she asked in a half serious tone.

"I'm all done playing for now, and everything for the rest of this evening will be serious and on the up and up, I promise." said Greg.

"Okay then, how do you feel about the Olive Greenery?" she asked.

"Sounds great! Let's go. Only let me drive, I want to test out the vehicle I rented, I may end up buying one of these things yet," said Greg with his hand over his heart.

Brandy furrowed her brows, not knowing what she was in for, but wondering what he was up to again. She was going to have to keep an eye on this one, he really was tricky.

Greg told her to wait at the entrance of the building, he would bring the ride around to her. Then he took off running and in no time, he drove up in a Red Lamborghini. *Oh my God!* Brandy thought. She had seen them, sure, but had never been in one.

"Now, here," he said, lifting up the vertical door, "Hop in and I will drive it this time, you aren't used to them and they can be very temperamental." *This time?* she thought, why would he say that? It isn't as though she was ever going to get a chance to drive it later. It wasn't even his after all, and those rental car companies were funny about letting people drive who were not listed.

He lifted the door up for her and she dropped herself in. These sporty cars were very low to the ground, especially for a woman in heels.

"Are we going somewhere fancy?" She asked him. "I just wanted to go to the Olive Greenery, they don't valet park, I'm pretty sure. How are you able to afford this?" asked Brandy, totally amused.

"Well, it's a rental of course." Greg replied.

"Right, a rental." She repeated back. But in her mind, she knew it wasn't. All the radio stations were preset to things he liked and he already knew which button to push to get which station. In fact, he was a bit too comfortable with the whole car and every button in it to have only driven it a few hours. AND it was red, his favorite color.

She didn't want to call him out on it, or call him a liar, but she wasn't buying that it was a rental. Why he was not being straight with her, she didn't know how, but this car belonged to this man! Of that she was sure. Brandy's intuition was in hyper drive. She hoped he was not into some crazy shit that was not legal.

He had been a perfect gentleman at dinner, pulling chairs, passing shared items, even buying their drinks, but she insisted on buying her own dinner. It was her habit to do on a first date. Greg pulled the car up to the door again. This time, he let her get her own car door.

Did that mean he was upset because she insisted on buying her own meal? Hopefully not. That would make him kind of male chauvinistic, and she didn't like that type. That was how Tray would have reacted.

Tray had to be "the man," meaning he had to be in charge and in control in every situation. This was the chief complaint she'd had about him, well, that and he cheated on her every five seconds.

11

The Conspiracy to Deceive

Brandy and Greg never did have the rest of their all- important conversation. But the need for having it was more Brandy needing to be in control of the situation anyway. It was a good thing for the relationship for her to turn over even some of the power and control, and doing so gradually was better for her as well. Time would answer any other questions. Time would clear up any issues, and clarify whatever still needed to be clarified. She would just wait it out.

Back at the apartment, she took her leftovers in to give to Lucy. Lucy had asked her to, and she knew that they would not taste as good the next day; salad didn't keep well overnight.

Brandy was truly hoping that they could have had the rest of their conversation, but somehow, the dinner went by without any mention of it at all. This had been odd, since she thought that was the reason for the dinner to begin with. Greg came in to Lucy's room.

"Hey sis, you mind getting out? We need to have a private conversation." He was of course joking and teasing his sister again. It was her room and she was not well enough to leave it. They busted up laughing.

Must have been a family thing, they knew when they were serious and when they were kidding, Brandy didn't know either of them well enough to tell that.

Through the sliding doors of her living room, Brandy could see that a decorative cloth and candle had been placed on her patio table. She wondered if this was another of Greg's plans.

She did however have some tricks up her sleeves for these two jokers. They had been getting the better of her for a while now, and she wanted badly to get back at them. It was in their nature, but it wasn't in hers to do so.

She would need to turn to an expert, someone to get the plan down right. But whom? She turned to Bill, their dad. He had been such a great sport the whole time he was staying there, and she knew he would be game.

How would she make that phone call without alerting her subjects? She knew! She would ask if anyone was up for a snack and offer to make it but be out of a key ingredient, and have to run to the store. That would let her get out of the house to place the call.

It worked like clockwork, and in just a few minutes she was on her way back to the apartment, canned milk and plan in hand. Bill had been keen on the plan from the first moment he heard of it.

Seems they liked to pull this kind of stuff at home a lot growing up, and did not consider him as sacred ground. He informed her that they both could dish it out, but did not take it very well, and that he was happy to arrange a scheme with her.

The scheme called for him to call the apartment forty-five minutes into the hour. She was to answer, and pretend it was a doctor from the hospital? No...she didn't want to worry them needlessly, maybe someone from her job?

Yes, that was it, someone from her job calling, a boss. And that he was sending Brandy away on a special assignment to Italy. Hmm, not impossible, not likely, but still plausible, and she had to leave the next day or miss out on the opportunity.

There, the plan was made. Back inside now, she took the milk into the kitchen, made the snack and went to sit down for a board game when the phone rang. "Wonder who it could be at this hour?" asked Brandy.

"Who would be calling this late?" chimed in Lucy. Brandy answered the phone. "Umm hmmm, umm hmm. No. Yes, of course. No? Okay, if I have to, sure I'll go." She had had a non-existent conversation with their dad on the other line. She then hung up the phone and in her best acting mode said: "Well guys, guess what? I have to leave in the morning to go to Italy for a business trip. It's mandatory."

"Greg are you gonna be okay taking care of Lucy here while I am gone for three days?"

"Three days! But we didn't even get to have our conversation or, I mean I-well, no. I mean, I can take care of Lucy. Sure." he said finally.

In all actuality, Greg had hoped to pop the question soon to Brandy, but one thing or another, or his nerves, kept preventing him from doing so.

"Excellent, all is going according to plan," thought Brandy. The Plan, as told to her by Mr. Bill Caldwell himself, their dad who would have the inside track on what got their goat, what really got on their nerves the most.

He had said that neither one of them really liked disorder, they had impeccable tastes she knew that, and did notice how they kept everything around them tidied and wiped off, but she didn't register that as odd as she was the same way. But she didn't have anyone pranking her at the moment, and they did!

These days, Lucy got up and out of the house for her morning walk by about 9 AM. It was likely Greg would go with her, since Brandy had added to her tale a car to pick her up and take her to the airport.

Once they were all out of the house, she would circle back around and get back in, just as Greg had done, only she was not going to plant notes, she was going to follow Mr. Caldwell's suggestions.

She removed the clothing from Greg's bag and unfolded them and refolded them opposite of what he had them. This would not matter much to the average person, true, but she had it on good authority that this would set Greg bonkers.

Next she balled up his socks, and she turned his t-shirts inside out. It wasn't anything dastardly, just enough to drive him mad. Then on a smaller scale, she did a few on Lucy as well. She had toned it way down for Lucy, as she didn't want to really cause her any discomfort or harm.

In Lucy's case, it mostly involved her dresser drawers, switching the sock drawer with the underclothes and the jeans with the shirts. Aggravating things.

She finished just in time. The walkers were returning and they had puzzled looks on their faces to see her there. "We thought you left, weren't you supposed to be on a plane right now, heading to Italy or something for your business trip?" asked Lucy

"Yeah, weren't you?" asked Greg a little more fiercely. He did not like messes, but he hated women who were not honest with him even more.

"It was called off, so I won't need to go now after all," she said. "Guess it was a false alarm." It seemed a bit much to go through for a simple trick, but they were so darned smart and so onto everything she did, places she went and every move she made, that she had to have a plan and a backup plan just to pull off even the simplest of pranks. Now she got to sit back and watch it unfurl.

It didn't take long before Lucy needed a fresh pair of socks and a clean outfit after walking. She went to get them from her dresser. "Hey, what is going on here? "Lucy cried out.

From the next room, she heard Greg yell, "Who's been in my stuff? Someone has been in my things!" He quickly checked the outside zippered compartment to see if it was still there. Whew, it was! No one had taken it. Thank God.

12

Ring, Ring, Hello?

The item Greg was so concerned about was of course the sapphire ring he had purchased the day he picked up his car. He had not rented the car after all, Brandy had deduced correctly, it was his. He also had not just bought it, he already had owned it for months back in France, but had had it shipped to London, and delivered to the airport.

He knew he was going to be picking the car up and would be able to go to the jewelry store that was in the airport. He had seen a ring there that he thought would be perfect for Brandy, despite not knowing or having planned out what would happen between them yet. He figured it never hurt to be prepared just in case.

What he did know was that she loved blue, and this ring had a round London Blue Sapphire center stone with round white diamonds all around it. It was truly beautiful. More of a cocktail ring than an engagement ring, but he had it on good authority that that was what she liked. Lucy had been with her one day window shopping, and Brandy had pointed it out. Lucy had shown and tried on a ring she had fancied too. Brandy had paid close attention to it, just in case she had call for that knowledge in the future.

Greg knew he had to have that ring for her, regardless if he gave her a proposal or not, he would be ready if and when the time came. He purchased it right then and there. That's when the rest of the plan came to him, and he made some phone calls and set things into motion. He had judged her finger to be a size 6 or 7, but knew she could always have it sized if need be.

He also knew that if she said yes, he would take her to Italy for the honeymoon. It didn't matter when, she was bound to love it. He had heard her say she had always wanted to go but hadn't been.

Personally, he could think of ten places right off the top of his head he would much prefer going and didn't see what was so special or great about Italy, but he had been everywhere, and she had not. I mean, it was pretty and certainly had its attractions. It just depended on what you had hoped to do there, and if Brandy said "yes", he had hoped to Honeymoon there.

He would get a hotel room at the one of the most lovely hotels he knew there, a place in Florence that visually would knock your socks off. She had mentioned wanting to stay at the Carnival of Venice, Luna Hotel Baglioni, but having seen it, he was sure there were some even nicer places he could afford.

Greg looked at the ring. God, he didn't want to have to wait to ask her. He was tired of looking for the right moment, right place, and the right woman, right everything. At least he knew the ring and the honeymoon would be perfect, and even the woman was a keeper. He went into the dining room where Brandy was sitting on a chair up to the table. Greg knew he was jumping the gun a bit, but he was impulsive like that, and he was positive this time that he could not do better.

He dropped to one knee and took her hand. "Brandy Marie Goshen, I am in love with you. I know I haven't known you for very long, but I am finding I have little to no patience lately. Will you marry me?" He then presented the sapphire and diamond ring to her.

"Wow, okay, wow. Well, let me say first of all that this is the most beautiful ring I have ever laid eyes on. Secondly, I am deeply touched and honored that you would consider me as marriage material, and I am in awe of your knowledge and your kindness Greg, but I am afraid at this time that I am going to have to turn you down. It's nothing personal against you. It's marriage in general that I have some issues with.

"You see, Tray and I were engaged back in the States. I was pregnant with his child, but ended up losing it. So the next time around, I just want it to be the real thing," she continued. "When I marry, I want it to be forever. I have known you for what? Three or four months at most. That is in no way long enough for us to know each other well enough to even consider marriage. I mean, God! We haven't even kissed yet! Let's just take things slowly. I am in no mad rush, are you?"

Greg then took her face in his hands and tenderly, slowly, and ever so gently kissed her forehead, then her eyes in turn, then her nose, and lastly her lips, where he lingered. She was glad she was already sitting, her legs would have given out underneath her if she had not been.

"We can go at whatever pace makes you most comfortable," said Greg. "I am not going anywhere."

Brandy was taken aback, she had not expected him to kiss her right then and there, and she simply meant that they had not progressed to that point in their relationship to kiss. She had had a wholesome and moral upbringing, and that did not happen on the second date, or third for that matter.

Greg could see he was having quite an effect on her. He smirked a little to himself, but inside, he liked that she had not been with a million guys. He was intentionally releasing his animal magnetism in tiny doses, but he was going to stop and soon of course. He was just enjoying himself a bit too much tormenting her. It was of course, all well intended.

Although theirs was an unusual situation (they had lived together now for almost four months) they only lived together in the strictest of terms. She as Lucy's roommate and he as Lucy's brother, they were bound to meet up sometime, it came down to probability, the Law of Averages or something.

Greg asked her to wear the ring and to keep it on until she felt they were ready to move forward in their relationship. Brandy agreed to do that. She did ensure that he understood that she was not saying a definite yes by wearing the ring. It was just a "so far so good" symbol, and a yes to their future of getting to know each other better.

With more talk under her belt with Lucy, Brandy had some ideas swirling around in her head. She was sure she was no prude, she had lived with her other boyfriends and they had, of course been intimate. But she had been afforded the opportunity to date them, to get to know them over time.

Coming to know someone was a gradual process and it took months if not years before you would be totally comfortable with another person, didn't it? Well it always had for her before. Not that she had been with all that many guys. In fact, if she actually sat and counted them up, she could arrive at a number. Wasn't that the ruler by which one determined if you were a player or not, if you could no longer count how many people you had been with?

She was often laughed at by her friends back home for her morals and her old fashioned ways, but having been raised primarily by her grandmother, that was just the way she did things, she knew no other way.

Although she had to admit, it did seem pretty wonderful and felt so right when Greg kissed her. She had not tried to stand yet since the kiss, and she was still feeling woozy. She wondered if her legs would hold her.

In all honesty, she had never been moved by a kiss or by a man the way she was by Greg, and she was by Greg, so much so that she only had to see him in the same room before she began to feel weak in the knees. There was definitely something different or special about this one, but just what, she was not yet sure. That was one of the questions she hoped to answer with time.

Brandy had never been one who'd had marriage as a dream or a goal growing up. Her's was a goal to write and to publish. Her's was a goal to accomplish her many lists of to-do items. Eventually she figured on settling down and maybe even having a few kids, but it was not in her immediate plans.

She knew she sure wouldn't be happy under a man's thumb or rule. If she ever did marry, it would have to be a partnership, a meeting of the minds, not a dictatorship. She was far too independent for that.

She felt a fierce and overwhelming need to protect and maintain her independence too. Would that need have to be sacrificed if she did marry? Time would tell, as it solved so many of life's issues, if only we learned to wait on it.

It Will All Come Out In the Wash

It was laundry day again. All parties in the household needed clean clothes in the worst way. As usual, Brandy was down in the laundry room, getting the loads started.

Lucy was doing better health-wise, but still was not well enough to carry baskets of laundry up and down the stairs yet. Fortunately, they had Greg to help with that.

Brandy meant to take off the ring before doing laundry, but she forgot. She sure didn't want to remove it outside of the apartment, but then, she didn't want to ruin it either.

Everyone in the building must have had today as their wash day. People kept coming in and seeing that there were no available machines and leaving.

Finally, Brandy was done with the washers and removed all her stuff. She was not happy with the amount of water left in one machine's clothes, it must not have spun well enough to get all the water out.

More people came and removed their laundry as well, then Lucy's friend, Alan, from down the hall who also worked at The Times, entered with his basket.

"Hey Alan, how are you? I wouldn't use that machine. It's not spinning well today," Brandy advised.

"Never does," chuckled Alan.

"So Alan, why don't I see you much at work anymore?" asked Brandy.

"Well, when paper sales declined and so many people lost their jobs and left, it left a lot of holes to fill. I ended up being relocated to a different department, and so I am not on your same floor anymore," said Alan.

"Oh, so that's why. Well, what area are you in now?" she asked.

"I am actually down on the first floor, across from where Lucy sits. I have my own office there. Speaking of Lucy, how is she? I never see her at work these days. Does she still work there?" he asked.

"Oh, yes, she just works from home now. They forwarded her phone lines to our place and she has a separate phone altogether to use for work." answered Brandy.

"Do you think she would be up for company any time in the near future?" he asked tentatively.

"Oh yes, she would love to see you. Come up anytime. Now even is good. Well, after you get your laundry done. We're ordering a pizza for dinner if you care to join us?" Brandy offered.

"Absolutely, but I will bring the drinks. I just bought some Coca-Cola and some beer," he added.

"Great, give us like a half hour then come anytime," said Brandy," I'm sure Lucy will be glad to see you, Alan." No sooner did Brandy get in the door than the phone rang. It was Bill, their dad. "*Bonjour Brandy, comment etes-vous ce soir?*" He had asked how she was this evening.

She didn't speak French very well, but was coming to understand it when read or spoken.

"I am doing well," she replied. "Thanks again for helping me prank the guys the other day. I think I got them both really well."

"Right, well, about that. I need to come clean on one thing. I was in on Greg's proposal the whole time, so when you asked me to help you, it just so happened to play into his plan as well," confessed Bill.

"Ohhh, were you now? Hmm, very interesting. You think you know who is on your side, but do you?" teased Brandy.

It was as Brandy handed the receiver over to Greg that she noticed the ring was missing off of her finger. She had not taken it off since she was...where?...The laundry room? Surely not...No. The bathroom? Maybe.

She ran casually to the bathroom as casually as someone can run. Once there, she frantically looked everywhere for the ring. No sign of it. *Oh no*! she thought. Where could it be? How could I have lost it this quickly? She knew she was going to need help finding it, and fast. But couldn't ask Greg! She went to Lucy's bedroom door and knocked. Lucy told her to come on in. Alan was there too, and they were talking. She hated to interrupt them, but this was an emergency!

Having explained her dilemma to them, she begged them for their help. "It isn't blue in the middle with diamonds around it, is it?" Alan asked.

"Yes! Tell me you have seen it!" she begged.

"I didn't know it was yours, but I found it in the laundry room earlier and I just took it to the apartment manager's office. She was going to call me if no one claimed it after a few weeks," he said. "She is probably still in her office if you go now, I just came from there."

Brandy flew to the manager's office. She pounded on the door, half knocking it down. "Did Alan...what the hell was his last name...just bring over a sapphire and diamond ring found in the laundry room? Here, I can show the proof of purchase. It's mine," stated Brandy, "he told me he had brought it in here to you."

She couldn't get that ring back on fast enough. "Oh thank you, thank you," she repeated to the apartment manager. "I just got this ring from..." She thought about what to call him. She had never referred to Greg as her boyfriend, let alone as her fiancé. Surely one or the other would be appropriate here, and she should know which.

When Brandy returned to their apartment, she heard the tail end of Alan asking Lucy out to dinner and a show for that Friday. Lucy accepted. She was feeling so, so much better these days. She had even mentioned the possibility of returning to work.

Greg too, had spoken to Brandy of looking for work there in London. Either that or making his virtual work a permanent arrangement with his company back in France where he imported and exported exotic and high end sports cars. This was a more likely scenario. He had definite plans to continue dating Brandy, and hoped to build a future with her as well, but gradually, slowly, and at her pace.

Both Lucy and Greg were up, Greg was in making breakfast. Alan was picking up Lucy for a walk in the park. Greg and Brandy had a day of sightseeing ahead of them as Brandy had yet to see most of what her new city had to offer. Brandy hopped in the shower to get ready. Upon soaping up, she noticed a small lump, smaller than a pea, in her left breast. A cold fear washed over her. "No, I couldn't have, it couldn't be, this isn't happening to me. What do I do now? How do I tell Greg if it is something to worry about?" Brandy looked down at her beautiful ring. "First things first," she thought.

ABOUT THE AUTHOR

Angela K. Lacey

This book goes out to all those who have helped me get this far in my dream, the "Real Caldwell family, whom I treasure dearly, to my dear friend and mentor John, and to my other dear friend John C. thank you for all the late night calls of encouragement. To my own family for their love and support, especially my mom, and lastly, to my son RP "puppy". I love you all.

I am a lover of people, a writer at heart, an over-user of commas, and a dreamer of dreams who just may be too idealistic to believe that there is ever a limit to what one can achieve if they never stop trying, believing, and learning.

As a survivor of Aqueductal Stenosis Hydrocephalus, I refuse to give in to any physical or mental handicaps, be they temporary or permanent, self-induced or inherent, real or imagined. I vow to renew, refresh, revive, and establish (or reestablish) my worth on this planet while yet there is still time, thereby renewing confidence in me and my abilities, in those who once believed in me as much as I do.

Cheers,
Angela

Printed in the United States
By Bookmasters